Princess Ponies
A Unicorn Adventure!

The Princess Ponies series

Princess Ponies

A Unicorn Adventure!

CHLOE RYDER

BLOOMSBURY

NEW YORK LONDON OXFORD NEW DELHI SYDNEY

First published in Great Britain in June 2013 by Bloomsbury Publishing Plc
Published in the United States of America in August 2014
by Bloomsbury Children's Books
www.bloomsbury.com

Bloomsbury is a registered trademark of Bloomsbury Publishing Plc

For information about permission to reproduce selections from this book, write to
Permissions, Bloomsbury Children's Books, 1385 Broadway, New York, New York 10018
Bloomsbury books may be purchased for business or promotional use. For information on
bulk purchases please contact Macmillan Corporate and Premium Sales Department at
specialmarkets@macmillan.com

Library of Congress Cataloging-in-Publication Data
Ryder, Chloe.
A unicorn adventure! / Chloe Ryder.
pages   cm.   — (Princess ponies ; 4)
Summary: To save the enchanted island of Chevalia, Pippa and her best friend,
a talking pony princess named Stardust, search for the missing magic horseshoes
in the haunted Cloud Forest, where they encounter singing unicorns.
ISBN 978-1-61963-294-3 (paperback) • ISBN 978-1-61963-295-0 (e-book)
[1. Ponies—Fiction. 2. Magic—Fiction. 3. Princesses—Fiction.
4. Unicorns—Fiction.] I. Title.
PZ7.R95898Un 2014   [Fic]—dc23   2013048652

Typeset by Hewer Text UK Ltd, Edinburgh
Printed in China by Leo Paper Products, Heshan, Guangdong
4 6 8 10 9 7 5

For Iyla, who inspired these adventures

With special thanks to Julie Sykes

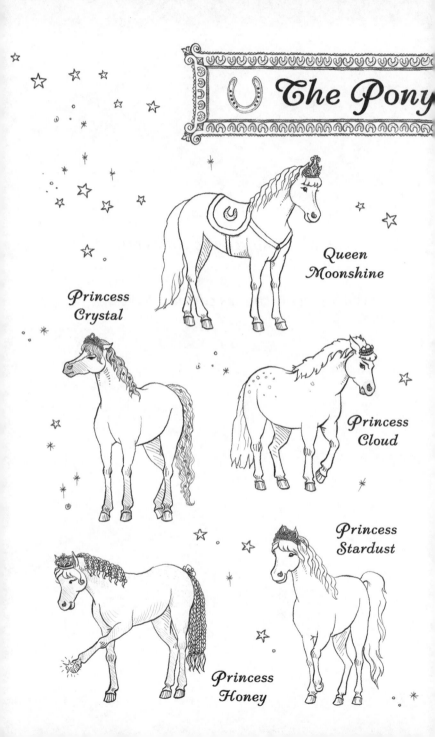

The Pony

Queen
Moonshine

Princess
Crystal

Princess
Cloud

Princess
Stardust

Princess
Honey

Royal Family

King
Firestar

Prince
Jet

Prince
Comet

Prince
Storm

Cloud
Forest

Volcano

Wild Forest

Stablesi
Castle

Chevalia

N
W E
S

Horseshoe Hills

Savannah

Grasslands

Canter's Prep School

Fields

Street

Early one morning, just before dawn, two ponies stood in an ancient court-yard, looking sadly at a stone wall.

"In all my life this wall has never been empty. I can't believe that the horse-shoes have been taken—and just before Midsummer Day too," said the stallion.

He was a handsome animal—a copper-colored pony, with strong legs and bright eyes, dressed in a royal red sash.

The mare was a dainty yet majestic palomino with a golden coat and a pure white tail that fell to the ground like a waterfall.

She whinnied softly. "We don't have much time to find them all."

With growing sadness the two ponies watched the night fade away and the sun rise. When the first ray of sunlight spread into the courtyard it lit up the wall, showing the imprints where the golden horseshoes should have been hanging.

"Midsummer Day is the longest day of the year," said the stallion quietly. "It's the time when our ancient horseshoes must renew their magical energy. If the horseshoes are still missing in eight days, then by nightfall on the eighth day, their magic will fade and our beautiful island will be no more."

Sighing heavily, he touched his nose to his queen's.

"Only a miracle can save us now," he said.

The queen dipped her head, the diamonds on her crown sparkling in the early morning light.

"Have faith," she said gently. "I sense that a miracle is coming."

Chapter 1

Pippa woke with sunlight warming her face and the sound of singing in her ears. The music reminded her of her big sister, Miranda, who often sang in the mornings. Miranda was mostly out of tune though, unlike the beautiful voices Pippa could hear now. Curious, she got out of bed.

"Stardust, are you awake?"

Princess Stardust's straw blanket was crumpled as if she'd gotten up in a hurry.

A wave of homesickness hit Pippa as she stared around the empty room. Annoying as Miranda was, she missed her—and Mom and her little brother, Jack. Did they miss Pippa too?

Four days ago Pippa and her family had been on a beach vacation when two giant seahorses had taken her to the enchanted island of Chevalia, a world inhabited by talking ponies. Pippa had learned that Chevalia was in terrible danger. The eight golden horseshoes that gave the island life had been stolen from the Whispering Wall, an ancient courtyard wall in Stableside Castle. If the horseshoes weren't hanging back on the wall in time for Midsummer Day, their magical energy couldn't be

renewed by the Midsummer s
Chevalia would fade away. To Pippa's
amazement, she had been asked to find
the missing horseshoes. Along with her
new best friend, a royal pony called
Princess Stardust, she'd managed to
find four of them, but Midsummer was
three days away and there were still
four horseshoes to find.

As Pippa got up, she remembered something important—Chevalia
existed in a magical bubble. No time
would pass in her world while she was
on the island, meaning that none of
her family would miss her. Pippa's
homesickness vanished immediately.

She skipped to the window to see
where the singing was coming from.

Princess Stardust's bedroom was in the smallest tower of the castle, topped with a pink flag, and it had a marvelous view. Pippa glanced at the sea sparkling in the distance before looking at the courtyard below.

"It's the Royal Court," she breathed.

All the ponies of the Royal Court were gathered together, with the princesses and princes in the front. Their colorful sashes and jeweled tiaras shimmered in the morning sun. Crystal, Stardust's bossy oldest sister, was conducting the singing with a riding crop, and the music made Pippa want to dance. When she had first arrived on Chevalia, Pippa had been so shy, but now she was starting to feel as if she belonged here and she couldn't wait to join them.

Pippa quickly put on the new outfit that had magically appeared overnight especially for her—a denim skirt, a striped T-shirt, leggings, and a sweat-shirt—then she hurried down the tower's spiral ramp.

"Excuse me," she whispered as she made her way to the front of the court-yard. The royal ponies smiled as they parted to let her through. "Thanks," she said.

Princess Honey was singing next to Stardust, tapping the ground in time to the music with a sparkly pink hoof. She was very pretty, with a shiny, straw-berry chestnut coat, but she couldn't

quite reach the higher notes, and her voice kept squeaking.

"You sound like a rusty stable door," Stardust said, laughing at her.

Honey hung her head.

"Hi, Stardust. Hi, Honey," Pippa whispered, squeezing between them. "What's going on?"

"We're rehearsing for the Royal Concert," Stardust replied. "We always hold it on Midsummer Day, to give thanks for Chevalia and the magical horseshoes. But Honey won't be allowed to sing if she keeps on making that racket." She playfully nudged her older sister.

Honey's brown eyes filled with tears. "You're so mean!" she said. Pushing past

Stardust, she trotted out of the court-
yard.

"There isn't going to be a concert if
we don't find the horseshoes," said
Pippa. "But before we start searching
for them, you'd better find Honey and
say sorry for hurting her feelings."

Stardust was surprised. "I was only
teasing. I didn't mean to upset her—I
forgot how much she wanted to sing
the solo."

Stardust was anxious to make it up
to her sister, so together they sneaked
out of the Royal Courtyard.

Once outside, she whinnied to Pippa,
"Get on my back."

Pippa jumped onto Stardust's snowy
white back, and they cantered off to
look for Honey.

"There she is," Pippa said, pointing, as they left the castle over the drawbridge.

"She's heading for the Grasslands," Stardust said, galloping after her.

Leaning forward like a racing jockey, Pippa buried her fingers in Stardust's mane. The pony galloped so fast that the air rushed at Pippa's face, making her eyes water and her hair stream out behind her in dark, wavy ribbons.

Honey didn't stop at the Grasslands but galloped on across the Savannah.

"Where's she going?" Pippa shouted.

"I don't know." Stardust sounded worried. "This is the way to the Cloud Forest, but she can't be going there."

"Why not?"

Stardust's stride faltered slightly. "Because it's haunted."

Pippa tightened her fingers on Stardust's mane, knowing that if Honey entered the haunted forest, she and Stardust would have to follow her.

"Faster," Pippa urged.

Stardust lunged forward.

"Honey, wait!" called Pippa. "Stardust has something to say to you."

They were almost at the edge of the Cloud Forest when Stardust finally caught up with Honey.

"I'm sorry," Stardust panted. Her sides were heaving and Pippa slid from her back to give her a chance to catch her breath. "I didn't mean to hurt your feelings."

"I can't sing either," Pippa confided. "I'm useless at it, and I get so shy I blush."

"You, shy!" Stardust and Honey exclaimed together.

Pippa nodded. "I'm very shy about lots of things, but Mom says if you pretend to be confident, then everyone will think you are."

Stardust was impressed. "That's great advice! I never guessed that you were shy about anything."

"So where were you going, Honey?" Pippa asked. "Have you got a secret hideaway?"

Honey blushed and shuffled her hooves. "Sort of," she admitted. "If I tell you the truth, you won't believe me."

"Why won't we believe you?" asked Pippa.

"It's a secret, so you have to promise not to tell anyone," Honey said. "I was going to see my friend Goldie. She lives in the Cloud Forest."

"No one lives in the Cloud Forest," said Stardust.

Honey took a deep breath. "She's a unicorn."

"A unicorn?" Pippa asked, surprised. "Unicorns are real?"

"Oh, please!" Stardust snorted with laughter, until she noticed that Pippa was glaring at her. "There's no such thing as a unicorn," she said. "Unicorns are make-believe—they only exist in bedtime stories for foals. Besides, you wouldn't dare go into the Cloud Forest—everyone knows it's haunted."

Just then a beautiful noise drifted toward them. As they stood and listened, Pippa wished her ears could prick up to detect sounds like Stardust's and Honey's.

"What's that?" she whispered.

"It's the ghosts!" neighed Stardust. "Hop on my back, Pippa. We should get out of here."

Now it was Honey's turn to laugh. "Oh, please!" she said. "There's no such thing as a ghost. That's the sound of the unicorns' song."

"It's beautiful," Pippa said, feeling herself soothed as if by a lullaby.

"It's amazing!" said Honey. "But I've never heard them sing together like that. We must find Goldie and see what's happening."

"No!" Stardust dug her hooves into the ground. "You can't go into the Cloud Forest. It's far too scary."

"I'm not scared," Honey said stubbornly.

"Wait!" Pippa said, as Stardust started to trot away. "If most ponies are too afraid to enter the Cloud Forest, doesn't that make it a perfect place to hide a horseshoe?"

Stardust stopped and stared at Pippa. "You're right," she agreed.

"Let's go then," Pippa said bravely. "We can look for horseshoes and singing unicorns at the same time."

Chapter 2

Stardust hesitated, but Pippa and Honey were already stepping toward the line of trees that marked the entrance to the Cloud Forest. A thick mist swirled around the trees, making it impossible to see more than a tail's length ahead. Pippa took tiny steps, squinting to try to see her way.

"Watch out," Honey called, tossing her red-brown mane.

Pippa stopped. A thick green bundle of vines, coarse like old rope, wound down from an enormous tree and blocked their way.

"Are they poisonous?" she asked.

"No, just heavy," Honey said, pushing them back with her nose as Pippa and Stardust joined her. "The first time I came here, the vines took me by surprise and I walked straight into them. You should have seen the bruise I got— it hurt for days."

"They're very easy to miss in this mist," said Pippa.

Pippa walked past the vines, holding them out of the way, then let them go when Stardust and Honey were clear.

"Vines like that could knock out an

elephant," Pippa giggled, watching them swing back across the path like a giant pendulum.

"What's an elephant?" Honey and Stardust asked together.

"Well," Pippa began, searching for the right words. "Elephants are much bigger than ponies, and have thick gray skin. They have long trunks that extend from their faces that they use to drink water."

"Now *that* sounds like a creature for a bedtime story!" said Honey.

"Not if you want a good night's sleep!" Stardust laughed. "They sound scary."

As they walked farther into the forest, the mist closed in behind them and seemed to swallow them up. Pippa stared around nervously, half expecting a dinosaur to lumber out of the over-sized trees. The ground was springy with a thick carpet of leaves. A huge, green plant grew everywhere, with leaves like airplane wings and vibrant red flowers.

"It's like an ancient forest," she whispered.

"It is an ancient forest," Honey whispered back.

"It smells wonderful." Stardust stopped to take a deep breath.

"Listen." Pippa tilted her head to one side. She could still hear voices singing in the distance, but now there was a new, burbling noise competing with them. "What is that?" she asked.

The sound was familiar but she couldn't figure out what it was.

Stardust tossed her head. "I can hear it too."

"It's a stream," said Honey. "The forest has lots of brooks and ponds. They're partly why everything grows so well here."

The ground became spongier as they followed the sound of the beautiful voices. Water oozed through Pippa's sandals, making her toes wet. Stardust daintily flicked her hooves, showering Pippa's legs with sparkling droplets of moisture. Pippa couldn't help giggling. The noise sounded out of place in the impressive forest, like laughing out loud in a library.

"That was cold!" she said.

"Sorry." Stardust hung back so that she didn't splash Pippa anymore.

The ground grew boggier until, finally, they reached a brook. It was small enough to jump. Honey went first, clearing it easily, then turned back and called for the others to join her.

Before Pippa could go anywhere though, something buzzed above her head, producing a breeze that lifted her hair and tickled her neck.

"Eeek!" Stardust whinnied, turning around.

Her eyes were wide with fright and she jumped, her brown hooves pawing at the air.

Pippa's mouth fell open. Dropping down on the leafy ground, she covered her head with her arms. A bird-sized creature darted overhead, red flames shooting from its mouth.

"Help! A dragon!" neighed Stardust.

Honey almost fell over her pink hooves laughing. "A *dragonfly*," she said. "Stand still and stop panicking.

26

Dragonflies won't hurt you, though accidents can happen if you get in their way."

Pippa's heart beat rapidly. It was all very well for Honey to tell them to stand still, but knowing what to do and actually doing it were two very different things. She slowly stood up and stroked Stardust's trembling neck. Stardust whinnied softly. The dragon-fly circled above them. In a whirl of electric-blue wings, it spun away.

Pippa exhaled in relief. "Wow!"

Chevalia was full of magical surprises. Yesterday she'd met talking horseflies, and now here was this amazing fire-breathing dragonfly. What would she see next?

The music was growing louder. It made Pippa think of tinkling raindrops and colorful rainbows sparkling in the sunshine. She hurried on, eager to discover where it was coming from. The mist began to thin out. In places it hovered around her waist so that she felt like she was swimming through it.

Pippa was so wrapped up in the magical surroundings and the sweet melody of the music that she almost missed the dog crossing the path ahead. It was only when Honey shouted out that she looked up.

"Goldie!" Honey called.

The creature bucked, kicking out its back legs, and Pippa realized it wasn't a dog at all. It looked more like a tiny pony, rose-tinted brown with a flowing blond tail.

Honey took off, galloping after her.

"Wait for us!" shouted Pippa and Stardust.

Pippa's heart hammered against her ribs as they raced into the trees after Honey. What if they lost her? How would they ever find their way back out of the enchanted Cloud Forest? Fallen branches snapped under her feet and damp leaves were kicked up in her face. Pippa pushed herself to run harder, determined not to be left behind.

After a long chase, she and Stardust burst into a small clearing carpeted with mossy flowers, their golden petals shining like the rising sun. Honey stood at the base of a tree, its trunk twisted with age. She was speaking softly to someone, and Pippa looked around to see who it was.

A low branch stretched, like a twiggy arm, from the tree into the clearing. Perched gracefully on the middle of the branch was the strange, rose-tinted brown pony. Its silky tail flowed down like a waterfall. It had soft brown eyes and a blond mane. Pippa couldn't help staring at the creature's forehead. She blinked but it was still there. The creature definitely had a gold spiraled horn in the middle of its forehead. Pippa's breath caught in her throat.

"A real unicorn," she whispered, blinking to check that she wasn't imagining the beautiful creature.

"This is Goldie," Honey said, turning around to face them.

"Hello," Goldie said, her voice like the tinkle of bells.

"Hello," Stardust said, curtsying.

Pippa curtsied on trembling legs.

Her voice stuck in her throat and she couldn't speak. The unicorn was a smaller, more delicate copy of Honey! Not wanting to be caught staring, Pippa lowered her eyes.

"Hello, Stardust. Hello, Pippa," said Goldie. "Honey's just been telling me all about you."

"Hello," Pippa said, finally finding her voice.

The unicorn was much smaller than she had expected—not that Pippa had ever expected to meet a real unicorn. But then she had never expected to meet giant seahorses or talking ponies either. On Chevalia it seemed that just about anything was possible.

Pippa was amazed by the tiny unicorn, her golden horn shining brightly in the patchy light of the forest. Pippa's gaze flicked to Honey. There was no denying it. Honey and Goldie were almost identical.

"I'm so glad you came today," Goldie continued in her sweet, tinkling voice. "Strange things have been happening here in the Cloud Forest. This morning when we sang our waking song, a tree sang back to us."

Honey was puzzled. "A tree sang back to you?" she asked.

Goldie nodded, dipping her head. "The others are still singing to it."

"A singing tree," Pippa wondered aloud. It sounded like magic—the sort of magic that might come from a very special horseshoe. "Where's this tree?" she asked. "Can you take us there?"

Goldie looked uncertain. "I could, but it's in the very heart of the forest. And my family might be surprised to see you—they've never seen a real live girl before. Are you sure you want to make the journey?"

"Yes," said Pippa. Turning to Star-dust, she explained her thinking about the magical horseshoe.

Stardust whinnied with excite-ment. "We must look at this tree!" she exclaimed. "Please, can you take us there?"

Goldie gracefully sprang down from the branch. "Yes, follow me."

Chapter 3

The deeper they went into the Cloud Forest, the scarier it became. Sometimes the mist swirled around them so thickly that it was impossible for Pippa to see her own feet. Shivering a little, she wondered what the royal ponies thought about their sudden departure from singing practice. Would they come looking for them if they failed to return?

The ancient trees were enormous, and branches brushed against her like gigantic spiderwebs. But with Goldie leading the way, her horn shining brightly in the gloom, Pippa's courage came back.

After a while she heard the roar of water. The trees thinned and they came to a huge, raging river of muddy brown water. Goldie stopped on the squishy bank and waited for everyone to catch up.

"We're not going to cross that, are we?" Stardust asked nervously.

"It's quite safe if you know how." Goldie tried to reassure them. "Follow me closely and only put your hooves where I put mine."

Stardust nudged Pippa's arm and asked, "Would you like to ride on my back?"

For a second Pippa was tempted, but it wasn't fair on Stardust to make her carry extra weight. She shook her head. "Thanks, but I don't mind walking."

"This way," Goldie said, moving upstream.

She stopped at a slender tree branch that had fallen into the river. Pippa eyed it carefully. The branch only reached halfway across the river.

"There are stepping-stones from the middle to the other side," Goldie said, easing her concern. She gracefully jumped onto the branch and walked to the middle. "Follow me," she called.

Honey went first, and Stardust made Pippa go next.

"So I can jump in and rescue you if you slip and fall in," she said, smiling.

"What if *you* fall in?" asked Pippa.

"I won't."

"Then I won't either," Pippa said.

She took a deep breath, then stepped onto the tree branch. It was slippery with spray from the river. Pippa hesitated. Then she remembered a PE class she'd had at school in which the teacher had asked them to walk along a low beam in the gym. "Find something to look at straight ahead," the teacher had told them. "Focus on that and don't look down."

With the teacher's words ringing in her ears, Pippa inched her way along the branch until she was balanced over the middle of the river. The next part was even scarier because Goldie was expecting her to step down onto a rock in the river. The water roared past with an angry hiss.

"It's easy," called Honey, who had already reached the other side.

Carefully, Pippa stepped off the branch and onto the first stepping-stone. She wobbled as she landed, but using her arms, she managed to regain her balance. After that it was simple. The stepping-stones were bigger than she'd thought, and she quickly made it to the other side.

"That was fun," Stardust said, jumping onto the bank beside her.

The mist was starting to thin out even more. Pippa stared around her, marveling at the beauty of the ancient woodland and the huge trees soaring above her. As Goldie wove through the forest, the singing grew louder. It rang in Pippa's ears and made her want to dance and skip. Goldie led them on, until she finally reached the biggest tree Pippa had ever seen. It had a tall, redwood trunk that was dented and grooved like a muddy track. Its branches stretched stiffly out with a fan of whispery green leaves. Circling the tree was a herd of tiny unicorns, their golden horns gleaming in the darkness. Their heads were held high and they were singing loudly.

Pippa gulped back tears. The music was so special it made her want to cry.

"Listen," Stardust whinnied softly. "Can you hear that?"

Pippa nodded. "The tree's singing back to the unicorns."

Every line the unicorns sang, the tree sang back to them like an echo.

"Isn't it marvelous?" Stardust's face glowed with excitement.

The unicorns clearly loved it too. They sang on, their voices high and pure.

Squinting, Pippa looked up the huge, red tree trunk. She was sure one of the golden horseshoes must be hidden in the branches, but where was it?

Suddenly she noticed that one of the singing unicorns was watching the ponies curiously. Pippa smiled, and the unicorn snorted and looked away. A few seconds later it looked again. Pippa stood very still. The unicorn stared at her; then, breaking the circle,

it cautiously trotted over. Pippa caught her breath. In the same way that Goldie and Honey were very similar, so were Stardust and this unicorn. The unicorn planted her hooves in the ground, swishing her snow-white tail as she stared up at Stardust.

"You're funny," she said.

"Excuse me?" stammered Stardust.

"Did your horn fall off? You look really silly without it."

Pippa tried not to laugh. That was just the sort of thing that Stardust often blurted out without meaning to. But Stardust wasn't laughing. Hanging her head, she pawed at the ground.

"I don't look silly, do I?" she whispered to Pippa.

"Of course not," Pippa replied.

"I'm sorry," the unicorn said quickly. "My name's Misty and I'm always putting my hoof in it. I didn't mean to hurt your feelings."

But Stardust was too upset to listen and began trotting away.

"Come back," Pippa said, hurrying after her. "Just because you don't look exactly like someone else doesn't mean you're funny or strange. It's not nice to tease others about the way they look, whether they're people, ponies, or unicorns. But I'm sure Misty didn't mean to be unkind. We all do things without thinking about the consequences. You know, like laughing at someone when she doesn't sing very well."

Stardust started to blush. "I understand," she said.

Pippa wrapped her arms around Stardust and gave her a big hug. As she pulled away, she noticed something shining in the branches above her. Pippa squinted at the redwood tree. Was she imagining things or . . . ?

"Stardust," she said, her voice squeaking with excitement, "what do you see up there?"

Stardust looked up to where Pippa was pointing and gasped. "A horseshoe!"

"It's the fifth one," Pippa said happily.

The horseshoe was resting on the edge of a huge, messy nest. It was a long way up. Pippa shivered. She was scared of heights, but she'd been learning to overcome her fear during the hunt for Chevalia's missing horseshoes. The tree looked easy to climb. There were lots of handholds on its rough trunk, and if she stood on Stardust's back, she could easily reach the lowest branch.

"What have you seen?" Misty asked, joining them.

Pippa quickly explained about the missing horseshoes and how the island of Chevalia couldn't survive if they weren't returned to the ancient court-yard wall in time for Midsummer.

"I see," Misty said doubtfully. "But you'll have to be careful."

"Why?" asked Stardust.

"That's not just any old nest. That nest belongs to a dragonfly."

Pippa and Stardust stared at each other in horror.

"What do we do now?" asked Stardust.

"There's only one thing we can do," Pippa said. "We need the horseshoe so I'll have to climb up and get it."

Chapter 4

For once Princess Stardust was at a loss for words.

"That's far too dangerous," she whinnied at last.

"We don't have a choice," Pippa said firmly. "Neither you nor Honey can climb up there."

"Definitely not," Honey agreed, anxiously glancing at her sparkly pink hoof gloss.

Worry lines creased Stardust's snow-white face. "Are you sure you want to do this?"

"Yes," said Pippa. The giant seahorses had brought her to Chevalia to save the island. She was the only human ever to go there. Many of the island ponies had been suspicious of her at first, but now they trusted her and were counting on her—she couldn't let them down.

Misty raised a hoof to show that the unicorns should pause for a moment in their circling of the tree.

Quickly, before her nerves got the better of her and she changed her mind, Pippa waved at Stardust to move closer. The dragonfly nest looked empty. If she was quick, she could grab the horse-shoe before the dragonfly returned.

"Please stand here, under this branch," Pippa said.

Reluctantly, Stardust stepped forward. "You don't have to do this—" she began.

"I do," Pippa said. She made an effort to sound cheerful, and knowing that Stardust was scared for her somehow made her feel braver.

Swinging herself onto the princess pony's back, she carefully stood up on it. Once Pippa had gotten her balance, she was able to reach up and grab the lowest branch of the tree. The rough bark bit into her hands, but Pippa gripped it tightly as she began to climb up the tree trunk. Before long she had

straddled the branch in the same way she would a pony. Relief made her feel light-headed.

"Easy-peasy lemon squeezy," she called down to Stardust.

"Lemon squeezy? Is that something humans drink?" Stardust asked.

"No," Pippa said.

"It must be what those elephants drink," Stardust explained to Honey.

Pippa was too out of breath to explain that it was just a rhyme.

She looked above her. There were only a few more branches to go before she reached the dragonfly nest. She tried to ignore the prickle of fear that was giving her goose bumps. Pulling herself up so that she was standing on the branch, she reached up for the next one. Pippa climbed slowly, checking that each branch could hold her weight before stepping on it. Every time she went higher, she worked out the best places to put her feet before she moved them.

Far below, Stardust and Honey were whinnying encouraging words. And softly in the background, the unicorns sang as they continued to circle the tree. Their lyrical voices gave Pippa courage, and, as the tree echoed their beautiful music, Pippa climbed faster and higher, until she was sitting on the branch directly below the dragonfly's nest. She was out of breath, and, even though she wanted to keep climbing, she made herself sit still until her heartbeat slowed.

"Are you all right?" called Stardust.

"Yes, thanks," Pippa shouted, glancing down at her friend.

Immediately she wished she hadn't looked down. The ground was much farther away than she'd expected. Stardust, Honey, Misty, Goldie, and the circle of unicorns were toy size. No wonder their singing seemed to be fading in comparison to the tree, which was loudly singing back to them. There was a sick feeling in Pippa's stomach, and she became dizzy. Unable to tear her eyes away from the ground, she realized the unicorns were all staring up at her. It was very scary. All at once it hit Pippa that she hadn't asked the unicorn herd's permission to climb their tree, but it was too late to ask now. She wondered if the unicorns realized that it was the horseshoe magic that was making the tree sing back to them. Nervously she wondered what they would say when she removed the horse-shoe and the tree stopped singing.

"Well, I'd better get on with it." Pippa took a deep breath and then sighed. Now that she'd stopped, she'd lost the urge to climb any higher. And she didn't want to climb back down either. She was tempted to just sit there for a little while.

"No—I can do this," she said firmly.

Quickly, before she could change her mind, she reached up for the last branch and pulled herself onto it. The nest, huge and untidy, reminded Pippa of the crows' nests high in the city trees at home. It was filled with four large, green, oval eggs. Pippa saw herself in the shimmering surface of the largest egg. The eggs were beautiful and seemed out of place in the scruffy nest. Pippa's heart lifted as she saw a sparkle of gold.

"The missing horseshoe!"

It was wedged between the largest egg and the side of the nest. When she leaned forward, the horseshoe was just within her reach. Wrapping one arm around the branch, Pippa stretched out her free hand . . . and froze.

"Oh no!" she gasped.

The eggs were moving. She watched in horror as long, jagged cracks ran across the eggs' smooth shells. The cracks grew and the eggs began to rock, then to split open. A chunk of shell the size of a marble landed on Pippa's hand.

"Ouch!"

The shell was hot! Pippa quickly flicked it away. A long, slim leg emerged from one of the eggs. It was soon followed by a second leg. The legs waved in the air. A loud snap startled Pippa, and she clung tightly to the branch as the egg cracked in two. A round head with two huge eyes looked around in surprise. More legs were appearing from the other eggs. Soon there were four heads and eight startled eyes peering out of the nest. The baby dragonflies kicked away the broken shells and slowly unfolded their delicate, tissue-like wings.

"Oh!" Pippa sighed, mesmerized by their beauty.

Each dragonfly had a different hue to its silvery body and wings. The largest was turquoise, the second largest was red, the third had a purple hue, and the smallest was pink. The colors sparkled in the weak rays of sunlight that had managed to filter through the thick canopy of trees.

Without meaning to, Pippa had leaned forward for a better view. A tiny roar, followed by a jet of orangey-red flames, made her jump back in alarm. Snatching at some leaves, Pippa stopped herself from falling. Now all four dragonflies were hissing fire. Pippa's nose twitched as she breathed in the sharp smell of smoke. To her left, a cluster of leaves was smoldering.

"Thank goodness for the mist," Pippa said, staring at the blackened leaves. The tree was too damp for it to burst into flames.

Because Pippa had pulled back from the nest, the dragonflies seemed to have forgotten about her and were now competing to see who could produce the longest stream of fire. Slowly Pippa edged closer again. All she had to do was grab the horseshoe while the dragonflies were busy playing. But the nest was too hot and there was no way she could reach the horseshoe without getting scorched. Disappointment almost overwhelmed her. She couldn't go back empty-handed. There had to be a way of getting the horseshoe! Pippa's thoughts were tangled like knotted string. Below her the unicorns were still singing. She let her thoughts drift as she listened to their music. Suddenly she had it—the solution to her problem! Trembling with excitement, she leaned out of the tree.

"Unicorns," she called down, "please can you sing me a lullaby?"

The unicorns stopped singing and stared up at Pippa with blank faces.

"A lullaby," she called again. "A song for bedtime. Something gentle . . ." She trailed off, feeling unnerved by the unicorns' collective stares.

Then one voice began singing. "*Hush, little dragonfly, stop that fire. Listen to the lullaby and you'll soon tire. Don't breathe flames, close your eyes. Go to sleep, good dragonflies.*"

"That's it, Misty!" Pippa exclaimed in delight.

Misty stopped singing and the tree began to sing back to her in the same soft tone.

"Now everyone join in," called Pippa. "Including you, Honey!"

When the tree finished, Misty started again, and this time Goldie and Stardust joined in. Honey opened her mouth, blushed, and quickly closed it. Stardust nudged her encouragingly. Honey looked uncertain but Stardust kept smiling, until at last, Honey joined in too.

Pippa smiled at her. It was good to see that Honey had overcome her fear of singing in public. The lullaby was making Pippa feel sleepy, but the dragonflies weren't listening. They were having too much fun huffing out streams of fire. Misty, Goldie, Stardust, and Honey sang on.

Pippa joined in with them. "*Hush, little dragonfly, stop that fire. . . .*"

Was it her imagination or were there more voices singing? Snatching a very quick look down, she was thrilled to see that all the unicorns had joined in. Soon their singing and the beautiful echo of the tree began to drown out the roars of the baby dragonflies.

"*Listen to the lullaby and you'll soon tire. . . .*" Pippa sang on.

The flames shooting from the nest were slowing down. The littlest dragonfly was swaying as if she could hardly keep her eyes open. As Pippa watched, she settled down with her head tucked under a pretty pink wing. The purple-winged dragonfly was next. Yawning sleepily, he lay down and within seconds he was snoring. The red dragonfly's head was nodding. Collapsing in the bottom of the nest, she closed her eyes. Only the turquoise dragonfly was left awake, roaring and spitting out red jets of flame. Suddenly he looked around. He seemed surprised to see he was the only baby who still wanted to play. With an angry snort and one last puff of fire, he snuggled down in the nest.

Instantly Pippa reached for the horseshoe. The dragonfly opened an eye and stared at her.

"Hush," she whispered, staying very still.

The dragonfly flapped his wings half-heartedly. Then he closed his eyes and fell asleep.

Pippa grabbed the horseshoe, wedged it in her pocket, and began the long climb back down the tree.

Chapter 5

As Pippa scrambled back down, Stardust positioned herself under the lowest branch.

"Thank you," said Pippa. It was such a relief to land on Stardust's back and slide safely to the ground.

"You were wonderful," Stardust said, nuzzling her nose against Pippa's neck.

"So were you . . . ," Pippa said, aware that it was now very quiet.

Misty was staring at her accusingly. "What have you done to our tree?" she challenged.

"Um," Pippa said weakly, knowing exactly what Misty meant.

"It's stopped singing! Listen." Misty hummed a bar of the lullaby and waited, her golden horn pointing at the tree as if inviting it to hum back to her.

The tree remained silent.

"You've hurt our tree," said Misty.

"No," Pippa said, pulling the horseshoe out of her pocket. "It's not my fault. You see, it's because of this horseshoe. It's magic—that's what made the tree sing. But the horseshoe doesn't belong here. We have to return it to the ancient Whispering Wall at Stableside

Castle before Midsummer Day or Chevalia will fade away."

"You didn't say that the tree would stop singing," Misty replied.

Behind her, the watching unicorns nodded in agreement.

Misty quickly tossed her head. There was a flash of gold and suddenly she was wearing the horseshoe on her horn. A loud cheer rang out, and the unicorns stomped their hooves.

Pippa stared at her empty hands and gasped.

"Give that back," Stardust said, walking up to Misty. "The horseshoe doesn't belong here."

"It does now. We unicorns love our singing tree. We're keeping the horseshoe."

Pippa didn't want to upset the unicorns, but she knew she had to get the horseshoe back to the Whispering Wall, for their own good and the good of Chevalia. She did some quick thinking, then went and stood between Stardust and Misty.

"Chevalia is your home too, and if you keep the golden horseshoe, then you will lose more than just this tree. The whole Cloud Forest will disappear. That's why you have to give the horseshoe back. But if you love to sing, how about singing with the royal ponies? Your voices are so beautiful, they could learn from you. You wouldn't even have to leave the Cloud Forest," she added quickly, as Misty started to protest. "We could ask the Royal Court to come here."

Misty turned her back on Pippa and spoke to her family in urgent whispers. Pippa strained her ears, trying to figure out what they were saying.

At last, Misty turned to Pippa and said, "They don't believe your story about royal ponies, a castle, and a wall that whispers. It all sounds like make-believe. They want me to keep the golden horseshoe, but if you bring the ponies of the Royal Court here to sing with us, then they would believe you."

Pippa hopped onto Stardust's back.

"We'll bring them here right away," she promised.

☆

Pippa was very glad that Honey was with them—she'd been to the Cloud Forest many times and had a good idea which way to go. But even Honey got lost in the large forest, and twice they had to retrace their hoofsteps.

It was lunchtime when they finally returned to the castle. Pippa's stomach grumbled as they made their way through the packed dining room. The rosy red apples piled in the feeding troughs looked delicious. There was no time to stop for food, though. With Stardust and Honey at her side, she made her way to the top of the room, where Queen Moonshine and King Firestar were eating from their golden trough.

Pippa, Stardust, and Honey curtsied.

"Your Majesties," Pippa began, "we're sorry for interrupting your lunch, but we have something important to ask."

Queen Moonshine pushed aside a large carrot. "Go on, my child," she said.

The dining room fell silent. Pippa's ears burned as she quickly explained in a loud, clear voice what had happened that morning.

When she'd finished, she heard Cinders snort and whisper loudly to her mother, Baroness Divine, "She expects us to believe that?"

Several other ponies added exclamations of disbelief. There were whinnies of "Make-believe!" and lots of laughter.

Pippa was angry. "It's true," she said, turning around to address the dining room. "Why would I make it up? Come to the Cloud Forest and see for yourselves." She paused to stare around the room. "If you're brave enough, that is."

The laughter turned to mutters. Pippa noticed Divine whispering something in Cinders's ear. Cinders nodded, and then she quietly left the room.

Pippa turned to Stardust. "I'm sorry," she began. "I tried my best—"

Someone was banging a hoof for

silence. A hush fell as Baroness Divine stood and addressed the dining room.

"I say we give the girl a chance. Maybe she is telling the truth. And if she isn't, well, maybe it's time she left the island." She stared at Pippa, her square face tilted, her brown eyes challenging.

Pippa stared back. Her heart was thumping so loudly she was amazed that no one else could hear it.

"Thank you, Baroness Divine," she said.

Divine nodded. "If Your Majesties agree, then I suggest we leave for the Cloud Forest immediately. And if the horseshoe isn't there, then Pippa must return to her home."

Pippa opened her mouth to protest

but thought better of it. Divine was challenging her. If she didn't agree to her terms, then Divine would accuse her of making the whole story up. But the story was true, and soon she'd be able to prove it.

"Pippa, are you happy to take us to the Cloud Forest?" asked Queen Moonshine.

"Yes, Your Majesty," Pippa said loudly.

"Then let us depart," said the queen.

☆

At first the royal ponies chatted noisily and there was lots of laughter as they trotted through the Grasslands and the Savannah. But as the Cloud Forest came into view, the procession slowed and the chatter died away. At the edge of the forest, Pippa, Stardust, and Honey waited for everyone else to catch up.

"Are we really going in?" grumbled Princess Cloud. "Hasn't the joke gone far enough?"

"It's not a joke," Pippa said quietly.

Even bossy Princess Crystal's eyes were round with fear. Her voice cracked when she asked, "Does *everyone* have to go in?"

"The unicorns are expecting the entire Royal Court," Stardust said impatiently. "Anyone who is too scared to enter can just wait here."

Many of the ponies were scared, but no one wanted to look like a coward. When Pippa stepped into the forest, they all followed. The responsibility weighed heavily on Pippa. Would they be able to find their way back to the unicorns? And would Misty honor her promise to return the golden horseshoe when the royal ponies appeared and sang?

Pippa led the procession of ponies through the mist, retracing her steps from the morning's adventure. As the giant tree finally came into sight, Pippa stared up its thick, redwood trunk to the dragonfly nest, from which a fountain of flames could be seen shooting out every now and again. Seeing the tree once more made her appreciate just how high it was, and knowing she had scaled it gave her a burst of courage.

The royal ponies stopped close to the base of the tree to stare openly at the unicorns. The unicorns stared back in silence. It was hard to say which party was most surprised to see the other. The unicorns and ponies had more in common than they realized, and there was no need for them to be afraid of one other. Then Pippa realized something and her mouth fell open. It wasn't just Honey and Goldie, and Stardust and Misty, who looked alike. The ponies all seemed to have a unicorn double, identical in every way except for their horns and sizes.

Nudging Stardust, Pippa whispered, "Look—every pony has a unicorn twin."

Princess Crystal had noticed this too. Soon she was moving around the tree, pairing the ponies up with their unicorn doubles. When everyone had a partner, Crystal and Petal, her unicorn twin, both raised a hoof and began to conduct.

The unicorns sang first, one line at a time, then waited for the ponies to sing back to them. Their voices complemented each other's so beautifully that the sound was even more wonderful than that of the singing tree. Stardust sang to Misty, Honey to Goldie, and Queen Moonshine to a magnificent unicorn with a tall, golden horn. There were even stocky unicorn equivalents of Cinders and Divine.

"That's so beautiful," Pippa said, swallowing a lump in her throat.

As the song ended and the voices faded away, Crystal and Petal bowed to each other.

Queen Moonshine stepped forward, curtsying to her unicorn double, who

was wearing a tiny gold crown decorated with purple daisies.

"I'm Moonshine, Queen of Chevalia," she said. "That was wonderful. We'd be honored if you would join us for the Royal Concert on Midsummer Day."

"I'm Sunrise, Queen of the Cloud Forest." The unicorn's voice tinkled like a mountain stream. "It would be our pleasure to host the concert here in the Cloud Forest."

The sound of hoofbeats jarred in Pippa's ears. Turning quickly, she saw two scruffy ponies darting away through the trees. An icy shiver ran down her spine. The ponies running away were Night Mares!

She called urgently to Misty, "Where's the magical horseshoe?"

"Here," Misty said, pointing her horn to a fallen log. Then she looked confused. "Where's it gone? I definitely left it there."

Pippa noticed Cinders and Divine sharing a smug smile.

"Divine, have you seen the horse-shoe?" asked Pippa.

"No, I'm afraid not," Divine replied. "Are you sure there was a horseshoe here? Or did you just make that up to get attention?"

The watching ponies shifted their hooves as they muttered among themselves.

"It *was* here," Stardust confirmed. "Maybe it fell off the log?"

"No," Pippa said grimly. "I just saw two Night Mares running away through the forest. They must have stolen the horseshoe while we were singing."

"More make-believe." Divine shook her head.

"Quick," cried Stardust. "Jump on my back, Pippa. We have to catch them!"

Pippa jumped onto Stardust's back

and hung on tight to her long white mane as the princess pony galloped after the Night Mares.

Chapter 6

A thick mist enveloped Stardust and Pippa as they raced through the Cloud Forest. Pippa looked around her, ducking frequently to avoid being snagged by low-hanging branches. The Night Mares had a head start but Stardust was fast—and much quicker at turning. She began to gain on them.

"Stop!" shouted Pippa. "Stop, you thieves!"

In the distance Pippa could hear the roar of the river. If Stardust could reach the stepping-stones before the Night Mares, there was a good chance they could get the horseshoe back.

"Faster." She leaned forward, urging Stardust on.

Mud and leaves were kicked up by Stardust's hooves. Her breath came out in snorts and her sides shook as she chased after the Night Mares. They were almost at the riverbank when she finally caught up with them. As she stopped, Pippa leaped from her back and ran toward the biggest of the scruffy ponies, who was carrying the golden horseshoe in its mouth. Its forelegs were in the water but it was hesitating.

"Which stone do I step on first? Lightning, can you remember?"

"Um," Lightning said, stretching out a hoof, then quickly pulling it back. "Are you sure we crossed here, Thunder? The river's very fast-flowing."

"Useless brother! Of course it was here," roared Thunder. "Why did the Mistress pair me with you for such an important mission?"

"Take that back. I'm not useless—I spotted the horseshoe," Lightning said, blocking Thunder's path.

"Get out of the way," Thunder growled, shoving past him.

"No!" Lightning whinnied in fright as he slipped on the muddy bank and fell, taking Thunder down with him.

There was a loud splash as the Night Mares landed in the river. The two brothers struggled to their hooves, their dark manes plastered to their faces. Pippa and Stardust roared with laughter as Thunder and Lightning splashed around. But the current was too strong, and suddenly they lost their balance and were swept away downstream. Pippa and Stardust stopped laughing then.

"We have to help them," cried Pippa.

"And save the horseshoe," Stardust added.

They hurried along the bank after the Night Mares. Willowy trees grew next to the river, and their long branches trailed in the water.

94

"Grab the branches!" Pippa called. She didn't want the thieves to escape with the horseshoe, but she certainly didn't want them to drown.

The Night Mares listened to Pippa and swam to the opposite bank, where, grabbing onto the branches, they pulled themselves out of the rushing water.

Pippa and Stardust stopped and stared at them in dismay. Still clinging onto the willowy branches, the Night Mares stood in the shallow water while they regained their breath.

"You can't catch us now," Lightning shouted excitedly.

Pippa heard hooves coming up behind her. Misty dashed past, stopping at the water's edge. She leaned down, dipped her horn in the water, then quickly stood up. Pippa's ears rang with a cracking sound as the river began to freeze over.

"What's happening?" she yelled over the creaks and groans of the water turning to ice.

"It's horn magic," Misty explained. "All unicorns have a magic horn, and they can do one special thing with it. My horn freezes water and melts it again."

Soon the river was a thick slab of smooth ice. The Night Mares were having trouble standing and leaned against each other for support. Thunder tried to climb onto the riverbank and lost his footing. He dropped the horseshoe, and it skidded across the ice into the middle of the frozen river. Each time he tried to go after it, his hooves slid in different directions.

Pippa ran toward the nearest tree. She climbed onto a willowy branch that was threaded with vines.

"Careful," shouted Stardust.

Pippa's heart raced as she grabbed a vine and swung on it like a rope. When she swung out over the river, she reached down for the horseshoe. Her fingers brushed the cold metal, but before she could pick it up, the vine swung her away out of reach. Pippa pushed herself back over the river. Gritting her teeth, she stretched as far as she could. Her fingers touched the horseshoe and curled around it. She quickly snatched it up.

"Hooray!" Stardust and Misty cheered as she swung back to the tree.

Misty dipped her head and touched the frozen river with her horn. With a groan, the ice split down the middle and started to melt. Muttering and

grumbling, the Night Mares waded through the slushy ice, climbed onto the opposite bank, and trotted away, their heads low.

Pippa threw her arms around Stardust and hugged her tight.

"We did it!"

Misty hung back, until Pippa put out an arm and drew her close. They were still hugging when a voice echoed behind them.

"Well done, everyone."

Pippa turned around to see Queen Moonshine leading the ponies and unicorns through the trees toward them.

She nuzzled Pippa's wavy brown hair with her nose. "You've been very brave. We should never have doubted you."

"Stardust and Misty were very brave too," Pippa said quickly.

"Yes, they were," Queen Moonshine agreed. "And now it's time to return to the castle. We must hang this fifth horseshoe back on the wall where it belongs before anything else happens to it." She turned to address the unicorns. "Please, would you all grant me the honor of joining us? We'd love you to stay with us and sing at our special Midsummer concert."

The unicorns shuffled awkwardly, until Misty stepped forward.

"Thank you. That would be a great honor for us too, but . . ." She hesitated. "We're unable to leave the Cloud Forest."

"Why?" Stardust blurted out, unable to hide her disappointment.

Misty still hesitated, blushing. "We've never left the forest before—we're too scared to. We know about the ghosts who live beyond the trees."

Pippa bit the inside of her lip to stop a smile. "We thought there were ghosts in the Cloud Forest until we met you, but there's no such thing." She pushed a damp curl out of her face. "And even if you are scared, you shouldn't let it stop you from doing the things you want. I was terri-fied when I climbed the tree and faced the baby dragonflies. Honey was scared when we all sang the lullaby together. The royal ponies were frightened to come into the Cloud Forest. But we all managed to conquer our fears."

"Please come," said Stardust. "Your voices are wonderful. It would be amazing if we could all sing together at the ancient Whispering Wall on Midsummer Day."

Misty looked thoughtful.

"I'll come if I can sing a duet with Honey," Goldie spoke up.

Honey shook her head sadly. "I'm sorry, but my voice isn't good enough for that."

"It would be if you practiced—and I can help you," replied Goldie.

"That's very brave of you," said Misty.

Honey pawed the ground. She took a

deep breath and quickly said, "Okay, I'll do it."

Misty touched her horn to Honey's, then she gracefully turned around to face the watching unicorns.

"These ponies have shown such courage by coming here today. And now Honey has shown even more bravery by agreeing to sing a duet with Goldie. Can you overcome your fears too?"

There were bright flashes of sunlight sparkling on golden horns as every unicorn dipped his or her head in agreement.

"Yes," they sang, their voices chiming like magical bells.

Misty nodded back at them proudly.

"Let's go to the castle," she said with a smile.

☆

The late afternoon air seemed to shimmer with the beautiful voices as unicorns and ponies stood together and practiced their singing before the Whispering Wall. Sun streamed into the courtyard, its long, glittering fingers brushing the four golden horseshoes already hanging on the wall, making them sparkle and glitter with magic.

As the voices soared, Pippa stepped forward and hung the fifth horseshoe on Misty. Her fingers tingled with magic as the golden horseshoe met the golden horn. There was a brilliant flash of light, and Pippa shielded her eyes with her hands. Misty stood up on her back hooves and placed the horseshoe on an empty black nail.

Pippa's smile was so wide she thought her face might split in two.

"Five horseshoes safe," she whispered to Stardust.

"Five," Stardust echoed happily. "There are only three left to find now. We're going to do this, aren't we?"

Midsummer was in two days. Pippa felt doubtful. Could they really find all the horseshoes by then?

The unicorns and ponies finished their song and started a new one. Their voices swelled in the air, carrying Pippa's doubts away.

She nodded her head. "Yes!" she said confidently. "Yes, we are."

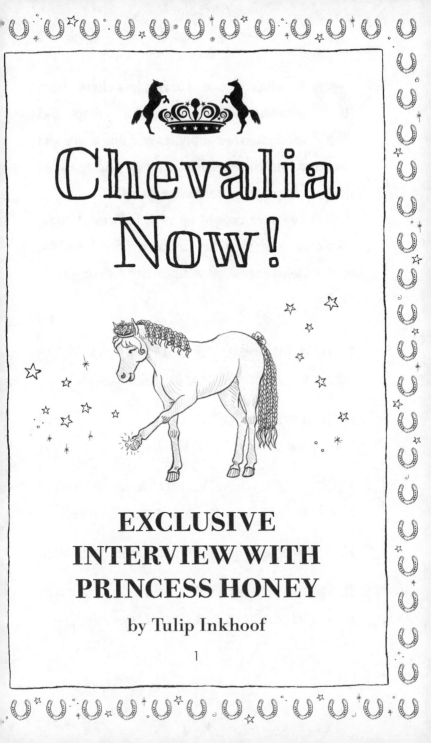

Chevalia Now!

EXCLUSIVE INTERVIEW WITH PRINCESS HONEY

by Tulip Inkhoof

Chevalia's Cloud Forest has long been thought to be haunted by ghosts. But today two brave ponies and one brave girl ventured into the mysterious forest and revealed its special secret: unicorns live there!

This reporter caught up with Princess Honey, who's been visiting her unicorn friend, Goldie, in the Cloud Forest ever since she was a young foal.

☆ **TI (Tulip Inkhoof):** Honey, how did you discover the secretive unicorns?

☆ **H (Honey):** First of all, can I just say that I *love* your purple hoof polish. It's so sparkly!

☆ **TI:** Oh, thank you—I visited the Mane Street Salon on my way to Stableside Castle.

☆ **H:** I love getting my hooves painted!

☆ **TI:** Me too! But let's talk about the unicorns. How did you find out about them?

☆ **H:** Right, down to business! Well, one day my class at Canter's Prep School went on a trip to the Savannah and I thought I could hear singing coming from the nearby Cloud Forest. As I trotted to the edge of the forest, I heard the loveliest songs floating out of it. I knew the legends about the forest, but these voices were so beautiful I didn't think they could possibly be ghosts, so I sneaked off and set hoof into the forest.

☆ **TI:** But weren't you frightened?

☆ **H:** Oh, I was, and I thought about turning around. Instead I sang back. I repeated the lovely song as I went into the mist—and I came face-to-face with a small unicorn!

3

☆ **TI:** How extraordinary!

☆ **H:** Mom and Dad used to tell us unicorn stories at bedtime, and I never thought they were real. But this unicorn was definitely real! She introduced herself as Goldie, and do you know what?

☆ **TI:** What?

☆ **H:** She looks a lot like me!

☆ **TI:** So you can confirm the rumor about the unicorn twins?

☆ **H:** Yes, all of the ponies on Chevalia have a unicorn that looks like them in the Cloud Forest. Even you, Tulip! It's a very special bond.

☆ **TI:** I wonder if my unicorn is an enterprising young reporter?

☆ **H:** Maybe! That first day in the forest, I met the unicorn twins for my entire family, but as the unicorns were so shy, I promised them I wouldn't reveal their secret. Every once in a while, especially if I was feeling sad or if the salon couldn't fit me in for a hoof scrub, I'd trot up to the Cloud Forest for a unicorn adventure.

☆ **TI:** So what happened to make you bring Stardust and Pippa with you today?

☆ **H:** I was upset because Stardust was making fun of my singing so I ran away to the Cloud Forest, and Stardust and Pippa followed without me realizing. Pippa thought that if everyone was scared of the forest, then that might make it a good

hiding place for the golden horseshoes—
and it turned out she was right!

☆ **TI:** I hear that Pippa rescued a horseshoe
from a dragonfly nest, and then it was
nearly stolen by two
Night Mares who
go by the names
of Thunder and
Lightning?

☆ **H:** Yes, the Night Mares were crossing the
river to get away from us, but Misty saved
the day with her magical horn by making
the river freeze.

☆ **TI:** What a busy day! Well, I should let you
get back to singing practice.

☆ **H:** Yes, Goldie and I need to practice our
duet for the Midsummer concert! See you
there!

Will Pippa and Princess Stardust
find all the golden horseshoes?

DON'T MISS THEIR NEXT ADVENTURE
WHEN THEY GET LOST IN THE WILD
FOREST AND RESCUE A PONY IN PERIL!

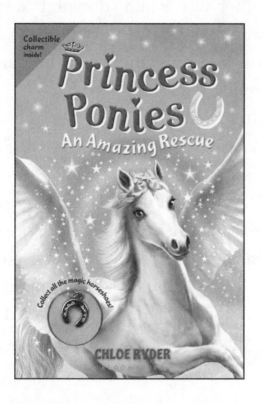

Turn the page to read a sneak peek . . .

Stardust trotted deeper into the forest. It was on the side of a steep hill and they were traveling downward, so Pippa had to lean back. The last time she'd been here with Stardust, they'd been going the other way. Riding downhill at speed was much trickier. Pippa didn't want to fall off and risk landing in the dangerous quick-stick mud.

After riding for a while, Pippa noticed a tree with a trunk that was twisted like a question mark.

"Haven't we passed that tree once already?" she asked.

Stardust glanced at it as she trotted past. "I don't think so," she replied.

"Well, we've definitely passed that tree there," Pippa said, pointing to a bleached-white tree trunk that stuck up in the air like a giant knitting needle.

Stardust stopped to examine the branchless tree. "Hmm," she said. "That's been hit by lightning. And you're right. We did pass it earlier." She turned in a slow circle, then stopped.

Pippa stared at the trees crowding in

on them. The Wild Forest was dark and gloomy. Fear prickled up her neck. Stardust seemed uneasy too. Her muscles twitched and suddenly she shivered. Pippa hung on tight as Stardust trembled.

Very quietly Stardust whinnied, "I think we're lost."